Do birds live in treehouses?

T0337553

Written by Rebecca Adlard

Illustrated by Camilla Galindo

Collins

What is in this book?

Listen and say

house

Download the audio at www.collins.co.uk/839673

treehouse

garden

Do birds
live in treehouses?

Lots of birds live in trees.

They do not live in treehouses.
I see lots of birds in this tree.

Birds live in nests.

Look! Three baby birds in a nest.

This is not a bird nest.
What animal lives here?

Look! Bees live here.

This is a beehive.

beehive

The beehives are in a garden.

Look! What is this animal?

It is a fox. It lives in a den under the tree.

fox

den

This is a donkey.

It lives in a stable.

stable

Wow! What is that?
What lives here?

This is a cave. A bat lives here.

cave

20

Picture dictionary

Listen and repeat

bee

beehive

cave

den

house

nest

stable

1 Look and match

 bee

 bat

 bird

2 Listen and say

Collins

Published by Collins
An imprint of HarperCollins*Publishers*
Westerhill Road
Bishopbriggs
Glasgow
G64 2QT

HarperCollins *Publishers*
Macken House,
39/40 Mayor Street Upper,
Dublin 1
D01 C9W8
Ireland

William Collins' dream of knowledge for all began with the publication of his first book in 1819.

A self-educated mill worker, he not only enriched millions of lives, but also founded a flourishing publishing house. Today, staying true to this spirit, Collins books are packed with inspiration, innovation and practical expertise. They place you at the centre of a world of possibility and give you exactly what you need to explore it.

© HarperCollins*Publishers* Limited 2020

10 9 8 7 6 5 4 3 2

ISBN 978-0-00-839673-2

Collins® and COBUILD® are registered trademarks of HarperCollins*Publishers* Limited

www.collins.co.uk/elt

British Library Cataloguing in Publication Data

A catalogue record for this publication is available from the British Library.

Author: Rebecca Adlard
Illustrator: Camilla Galindo (Beehive)
Series editor: Rebecca Adlard
Publishing manager: Lisa Todd
Product managers: Jennifer Hall and Caroline Green
In-house editor: Alma Puts Keren
Project manager: Emily Hooton
Editor: Emma Wilkinson
Proofreaders: Natalie Murray and Michael Lamb
Cover designer: Kevin Robbins
Typesetter: 2Hoots Publishing Services Ltd
Audio produced by id audio, London
Reading guide author: Emma Wilkinson
Production controller: Rachel Weaver
Printed and bound by: Pureprint, UK

MIX
Paper | Supporting responsible forestry
FSC
www.fsc.org
FSC™ C007454

This book contains FSC™ certified paper and other controlled sources to ensure responsible forest management.

For more information visit: www.harpercollins.co.uk/green

Download the audio for this book and a reading guide for parents and teachers at www.collins.co.uk/839673